Moo and Moo and Can You Guess Who?

STORY BY Jane Millton ILLUSTRATED BY Deborah Hinde

ALLEN & UNWIN
SYDNEY • MELBOURNE • AUCKLAND • LONDON

Can you remember Moo and Moo?
And do you remember that little calf too?
They're still on the farm, eating grass and clover.
I'll tell you their story – that quake is over!

The little calf too has grown up now,
Away from her mother, the Hereford cow.
She lives with the yearlings, eating fodder beet and hay
In a paddock by the creek, over the way.

Moo and Moo are lifelong friends.
They often moo about their happy end.
They go back now and then to that place on the hill,
And look beyond the grass at the massive limestone spill.

The cows have wintered well in the valley on the flat.
Their tummies are rounded . . . and they're looking very fat!
Inside each tummy, soon to be born,
Is a growing little calf, all curled up and warm.

A heifer or a bull? We'll have to wait and see.
Moo might have twins, and then there would be three!
Do you think the calf will have a spot on its face?
Just like its mother, who lives at this place.

Nine months on since that night in November,
Spring is near and it's almost September.
Moo and Moo are going to give birth.
A miracle, really, after that shaking of the earth.

While the other cows are resting one fresh and frosty night,
Moo moves by a tree and lies down out of sight.
She feels a little flutter and a tickle in her tummy
And she knows this is a sign that she soon will be a mummy.

After some time, with a push she delivers
A little bull calf who splutters, shakes and shivers.
Moo then stands up and proudly licks her little one,
And sighs with relief – that job is now done!

The little calf nuzzles and finds her warm udder full.
He suckles on her teats with a strong and hungry pull.
Warm and frothy milk on a fresh and frosty morn.
He's a happy little fellow, delighted to be born!

Daybreak dawns, and Moo looks around.
The birds are just waking, and their morning chorus sounds.
Moo moos to her calf, "I can't find my friend!"
And she searches the whole paddock from the start to the end.

Moo looks and she looks . . . then in the distance she spots Moo,
And following behind her is a little calf too!
What a happy, happy day – both cows giving birth together.
They are best friends now and will be forever.

“What shall we call our babies?” moos Moo with a laugh,
As they lovingly look at each other’s little calf.
“I’ll call mine Moo. And what about you?”
“I too am thinking Moo – named after you!”

So now we have Moo and Moo and the bigger calf too,
And our brand-new little ones: Baby Moo and Baby Moo.
All five Moos – old, young and very, very new –
Living in the Clarence Valley, and just loving that view!

Moo and Moo and the little calf too have been living happily at their home in the Clarence Valley since the big earthquake that struck the South Island of New Zealand at two minutes after midnight on Monday 14 November 2016. (If you haven't already read the story of how the two brave cows and the little calf survived the Kaikōura earthquake, you can do so in *Moo and Moo and the Little Calf too*!)

Some new words . . .

Here are some words about cows and their new babies that you might not have heard before. This is what they mean.

Bull: A male cattle beast of any age. An older bull is the father or sire of a calf.

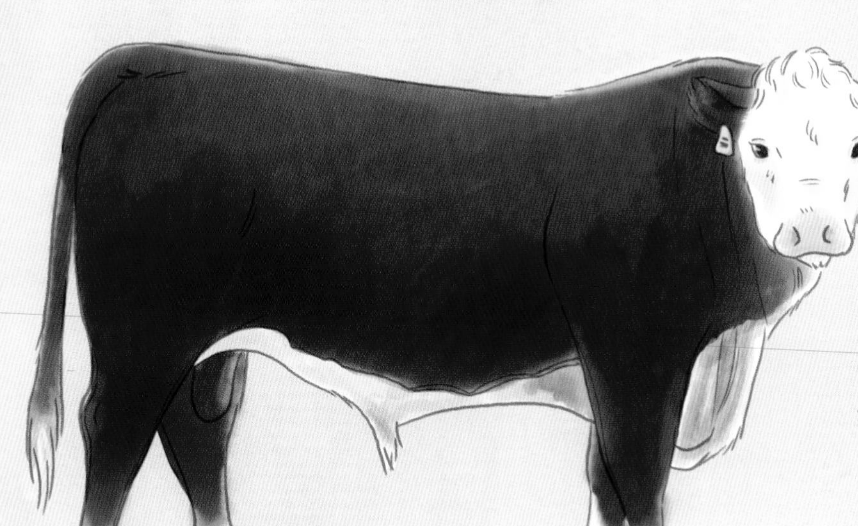

Calf: A young cattle beast. A female calf is called a heifer calf and a male calf is called a bull calf. When a calf is a year old it's called a yearling.

Cattle beast: Calves, cows, bulls and heifers are all cattle beast.

Hereford: A breed of cattle beast that's red-brown in colour with a white face and white markings.

Heifer: A young female cattle beast who will not give birth to a calf until she is two or sometimes even three years old.

Cow: A female cattle beast over two years old. A cow will usually give birth to a calf every year.

What cattle eat

Clover: A plant that grows after winter, as the ground warms up. Clover often grows with grass and this is called pasture. Cattle eat pasture.

Crop: Plants that farmers grow to feed to animals.

Fodder beet: This is a nutritious crop that grows very well. Farmers plant (or sow) it in the summer, then feed it to animals during the colder winter months. Cattle are fed a small amount each day along with hay and fresh grass. Fodder beet has a large yellow bulb, a leafy top and tastes sweet. Cattle love it!

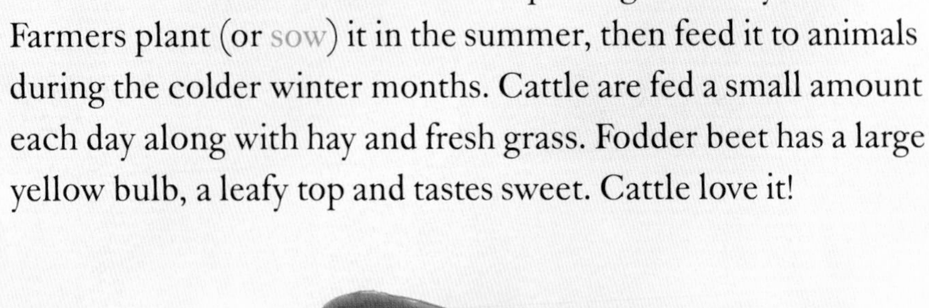

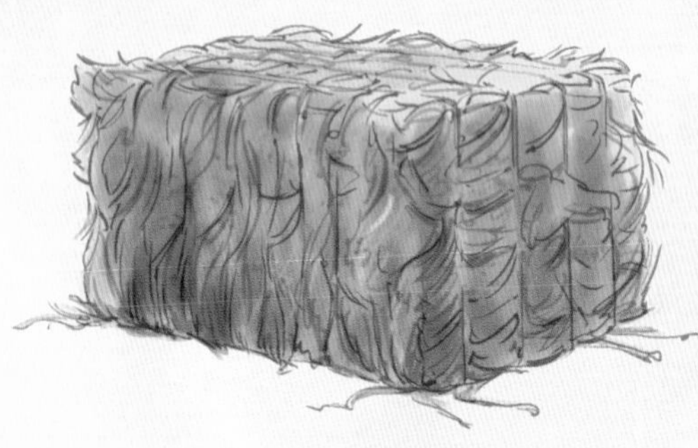

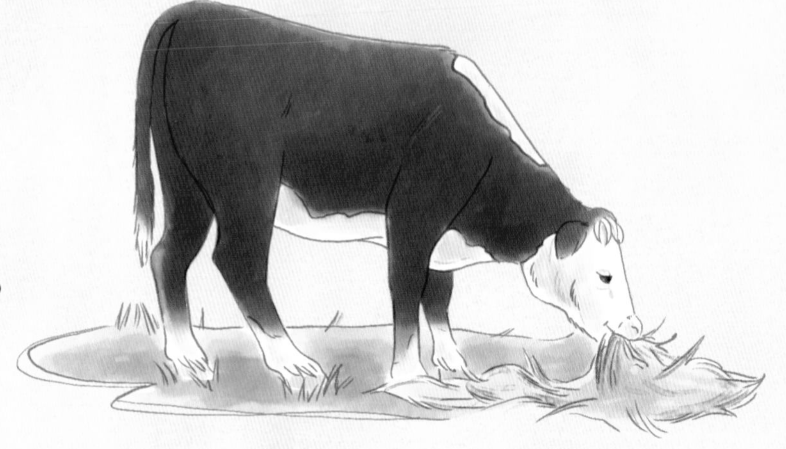

Hay: Grass that has been cut, dried, raked and put into bales, then stored in a shed. It is fed to animals in the winter, when the ground is too cold for enough grass and clover to grow.

Did you know?

- It usually takes about 280 days, or just over nine months, for a little calf to grow and be born – that's only a little bit longer than it takes for a human baby to grow!
- Like many other animals, a cow will find a quiet spot away from other animals to give birth. Most calves are born within four hours of the time a cow first feels the "little flutter and a tickle" in her tummy that tells her she's about to give birth.

- As soon as her calf is born, the cow will lick and nuzzle it to encourage it to drink her milk. A cow forms a very close and special bond with her calf. This is referred to as mothering.
- The newborn calf will stand up very soon after it is born so that it can reach its mother's udder. A cow's udder is found between her back legs and is where her milk comes from.
- The first milk a cow produces when her calf is born is called colostrum, and it is yellower and thicker than the milk that we drink. Colostrum is very good for the newborn calf, because it contains lots of important things to ensure the calf will be healthy.

To M. and T. and their own little Moo. D.H.

To everyone, young and old, who has read and enjoyed *Moo and Moo and the Little Calf too*. And to another little Moo, due for us too. J.M.

First published in 2017

Allen & Unwin
Level 3, 228 Queen Street
Auckland 1010, New Zealand
Phone: (64 9) 377 3800

Email: info@allenandunwin.com
Web: www.allenandunwin.co.nz

83 Alexander Street
Crows Nest NSW 2065, Australia
Phone: (61 2) 8425 0100

A catalogue record for this book is available from the National Library of New Zealand

ISBN 978 1 760631 61 1

Design by Kate Barraclough
Set in 17/23 pt Founders Caslon
Printed and bound in China by Hang Tai Printing Company Limited

10 9 8 7 6 5 4 3 2 1